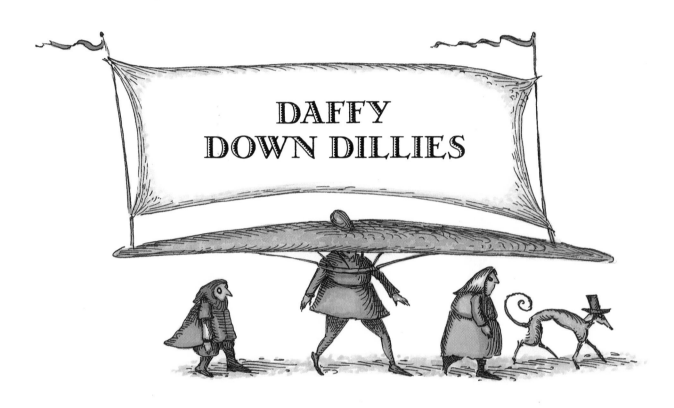

DAFFY
DOWN DILLIES

For Tess
—J. O'B.

Copyright © 1992 by John O'Brien
All rights reserved
Published by Caroline House
Boyds Mills Press, Inc.
A Highlights Company
910 Church Street
Honesdale, Pennsylvania 18431

Publisher Cataloging-in-Publication Data
Lear, Edward, 1812-1888.
Daffy down dillies : silly limericks / by Edward Lear ; illustrated
by John O'Brien
[32] p. : col. ill. ; cm.
Summary: A collection of limericks comically illustrated.
ISBN 1-56397-007-4
1. Nonsense-verses, English. 2. Children's poetry, English.
3. Limericks, Juvenile. [1. Nonsense-verses. 2. English poetry
3. Limericks.]
I. O'Brien, John., ill. II. Title.
821/.8—dc20   1992
Library of Congress Card Number: 91-72986

First edition, 1992
Book designed by Katy Riegel
Distributed by St. Martin's Press
Printed in the United States of America

Illustrated by
JOHN O'BRIEN

DAFFY DOWN DILLIES

SILLY LIMERICKS
by
EDWARD LEAR

CAROLINE HOUSE

There was an old man of West Dumpet,
Who possessed a large nose like a trumpet.
When he blew it aloud, it astonished the crowd,
And was heard through the whole of West Dumpet.

There was an old man of Messina,
Whose daughter was named Opsibeena.
She wore a small wig, and rode out on a pig,
To the perfect delight of Messina.

There was an old person of Minety
Who purchased five hundred and ninety
Large apples and pears, which he threw unawares,
At the heads of the people of Minety.

There was an old person of Spain,
Who hated all trouble and pain.
So he sat on a chair,
    with his feet in the air,
That umbrageous old person of Spain.

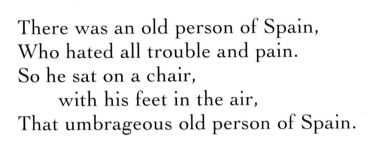

There was an old person of Hurst,
Who drank when he was not athirst.
When they said, "You'll grow fatter,"
    he answered, "What matter?"
That globular person of Hurst.

There is a young lady, whose nose,
Continually prospers and grows.
When it grew out of sight, she exclaimed in a fright,
"Oh! Farewell to the end of my nose!"

There was an old person of Mold,
Who shrank from sensations of cold;
So he purchased some muffs,
    some furs and some fluffs,
And wrapped himself from the cold.

There was an old man with a flute,
A serpent ran into his boot;
But he played day and night,
    till the serpent took flight,
And avoided that man with a flute.

There was a young lady of Clare,
Who was sadly pursued by a bear.
When she found she was tired,
  she abruptly expired,
That unfortunate lady of Clare.

There was a young lady of Hull,
Who was chased by a virulent bull;
But she seized on a spade, and called out—"Who's afraid!"
Which distracted that virulent bull.

There was an old person of Dean,
Who dined on one pea, and one bean.
For he said, "More than that, would make me too fat,"
That cautious old person of Dean.

There was an old person of Slough,
Who danced at the end of a bough;
But they said, "If you sneeze,
  you might damage the trees,
You imprudent old person of Slough."

There was an old man of Aôsta,
Who possessed a large cow, but he lost her.
But they said, "Don't you see,
  she has rushed up a tree?
You invidious old man of Aôsta!"

There was an old man with a beard,
Who said, "It is just as I feared! —
Two owls and a hen,
    four larks and a wren,
Have all built their nests in my beard!"

There was an old man of Dee-side
Whose hat was exceedingly wide,
But he said, "Do not fail,
    if it happen to hail,
To come under my hat at Dee-side!"

There was an old man who said,
"How—shall I flee from this horrible cow?
I will sit on this stile,
    and continue to smile,
Which may soften the heart of that cow."

There was an old man of El Hums,
Who lived upon nothing but crumbs,
Which he picked off the ground,
    with the other birds round,
In the roads and the lanes of El Hums.

There was an old man, who when little
Fell casually into a kettle.
But growing too stout,
    he could never get out,
So he passed all his life in that kettle.

There was an old man who said, "Hush!
I perceive a young bird in this bush!"
When they said, "Is it small?"
        he replied, "Not at all!
It is four times as big as the bush!"

There was an old man of Dumbree,
Who taught little owls to drink tea.
For he said, "To eat mice, is not proper or nice,"
That amiable man of Dumbree.

There was an old man of Moldavia,
Who had the most curious behavior;
For while he was able, he slept on a table,
That funny old man of Moldavia.

There was an old man in a boat,
Who said, "I'm afloat! I'm afloat!"
When they said, "No! you ain't!" he was ready to faint,
That unhappy old man in a boat.

There was an old man of the Coast,
Who placidly sat on a post.
But when it was cold,
    he relinquished his hold,
And called for some hot buttered toast.

There was an old man of Dunluce,
Who went out to sea on a goose.
When he'd gone out a mile,
    he observed with a smile,
"It is time to return to Dunluce."

There was a young person of Ayr,
Whose head was remarkably square:
On the top, in fine weather, she wore a gold feather,
Which dazzled the people of Ayr.

There was a young lady whose bonnet,
Came untied when the birds sat upon it.
But she said, "I don't care! All the birds in the air
Are welcome to sit on my bonnet!"

There was an old man of the West,
Who wore a pale plum-colored vest.
When they said, "Does it fit?"
  he replied, "Not a bit!"
That uneasy old man of the West.

There was an old person of Ware,
Who rode on the back of a bear.
When they asked,—"Does it trot?"—
  he said, "Certainly not!
He's a Moppsikon Floppsikon bear!"

There was an old person of Wilts,
Who constantly walked upon stilts.
He wreathed them with lilies,
　　and daffy-down-dillies,
That elegant person of Wilts.

There was an old man of the North,
Who fell into a basin of broth.
But a laudable cook, fished him out with a hook,
Which saved that old man of the North.

There was an old person of Ewell,
Who chiefly subsisted on gruel.
But to make it more nice,
   he inserted some mice,
Which refreshed that old person of Ewell.

There was an old person of Skye,
Who waltzed with a Bluebottle fly:
They buzzed a sweet tune,
    to the light of the moon,
And entranced all the people of Skye.

There was an old man of the Hague,
Whose ideas were excessively vague.
He built a balloon, to examine the moon,
That deluded old man of the Hague.

There was an old person of Tring,
Who embellished his nose with a ring.
He gazed at the moon,
    every evening in June,
That ecstatic old person of Tring.

There was an old person of Nice,
Whose associates were usually geese.
They walked out together,
    in all sorts of weather,
That affable person of Nice!

There was a young person in green,
Who seldom was fit to be seen.
She wore a long shawl,
    over bonnet and all,
Which enveloped that person in green.

There was an old man, on whose nose,
Most birds of the air could repose.
But they all flew away, at the closing of day,
Which relieved that old man and his nose.

THE END